Arthur Starter Book 02

ARTHUR

and the Dog Show

KB032644

by Marc Brown

Long tail Books

Annual
ELWOOD CITY
DOG
SHOW
LINCOLN PARK
Saturday
2 PM

“Look, Pal!” said Arthur. “There’s going to be a dog show on Saturday. We should enter. Maybe we’ll win a prize.”

Arthur took Pal out to the backyard. "If we want to do well, we have to practice. So, roll over, Pal."

Pal wagged his tail.

"Roll over!" Arthur said again.

Pal wagged his tail harder.

"Maybe we should start with something easier," said Arthur. "Sit, Pal!"

Pal began digging a hole.

"No, no," said Arthur. "Like this."
Pal ran around him in circles.
"This will be harder than I thought," Arthur said.
"We need to practice."

Every day they practiced

and practiced

and practiced.

On the day of the show, Arthur got up early.
He gave Pal a bath and a good brushing.
"You need to look your best in the winner's circle," he explained.

There were lots of dogs at the dog show.
Some of them were all dressed up.
"Don't worry, Pal," said Arthur. "We'll show them."

REGISTRATION
2

When it was Arthur's turn, he led Pal into the ring.
"Sit, Pal," he said.
Pal rolled over.

"Wag your tail, Pal!" Arthur ordered.
Pal stood up on his back legs.
The judges did not look pleased.

At the end, Arthur didn't even look at Pal's score.
"It can't be good," he said. "All that work for nothing."

JUDGES
1
3

Pal came over and sniffed at Arthur, but Arthur didn't move.
So Pal began licking Arthur's face.
"Stop that, Pal. It tickles."
But Pal didn't stop. He kept licking and licking
until Arthur started to smile.

JUDGES
TUCKER

"You're right," Arthur said.
"It's not the end of the world. Come on, let's go home."
Arthur started to leave, but the judges stopped him.

JUDGE
JUDGE
TUCKER
ELIZA

And then they declared Pal a winner!